What I See

What I

Holly Keller

Green Light Readers
Harcourt, Inc.
Orlando   Austin   New York   San Diego   Toronto   London

See

I see a rose.

I see a nose.

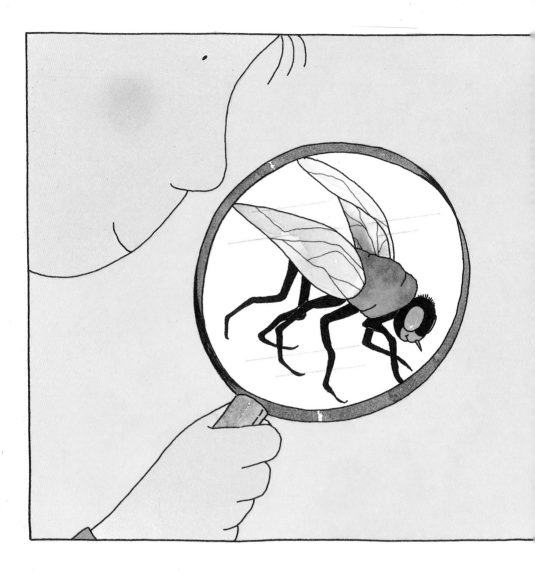

I see a fly.

I see a pie.

I see a cat.

I see a mat.

I see a top.

I see a mop.

I see a dog.

I see a frog.

I see a bee.

I see me!

What Do You See?

Make a shape with paint.

mask

spider

two horses

WHAT YOU'LL NEED

paper

paint

brushes

Fold the paper in half.

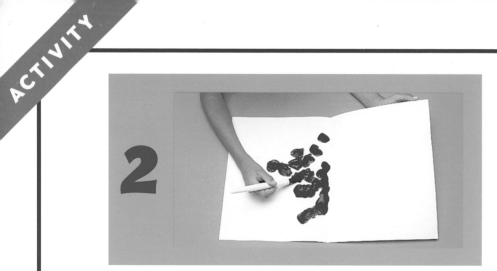

2

Put paint on one side of the paper.

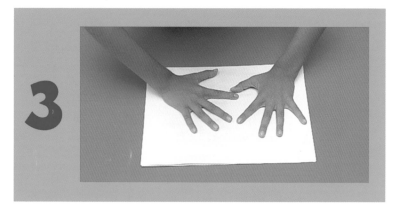

3

Close the paper. Press hard.
Open the paper.

What do you see?
Ask your friends
what they see.

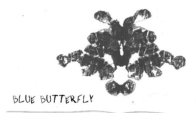

BLUE BUTTERFLY

Your Own Camera

Be a photographer and take pictures of what you see!

WHAT YOU'LL NEED

paper   markers or crayons   tape

1 Fold a piece of paper in half. Tape the sides.

2 Make it look like a real camera.

3 Draw some pictures. Put them inside your camera.

4 Share your pictures with your friends!

Meet the Author-Illustrator

Dear Boys and Girls,

When I am home, I love to go on walks around the pond. I thought of my walks when I wrote *What I See*, because I see so many things. I know every squirrel that lives by me.

Just for fun, I hid some things in the pictures of *What I See*. Can you find them? What do you see?

Holly Keller

www.HarcourtBooks.com

First Green Light Readers edition 1999
Green Light Readers is a trademark of Harcourt, Inc., registered in the
United States of America and/or other jurisdictions.

The Library of Congress has cataloged an earlier edition as follows:
Keller, Holly.
What I see/Holly Keller.
p. cm.
"Green Light Readers."
Summary: Illustrations and simple rhyming text
describe what a child sees around the house and garden.
[1. Stories in rhyme.] I. Title.
PZ8.3.K275Wh 1999
[E]—dc21 98-17519
ISBN 0-15-204814-6
ISBN 0-15-204854-5 (pb)

LEO 10 9 8 7 6 5
4500208595

Ages 4-6
Grades: K-1
Guided Reading Level: C
Reading Recovery Level: 3

Green Light Readers
For the reader who's ready to GO!

"A must-have for any family with a beginning reader."—*Boston Sunday Herald*

"You can't go wrong with adding several copies of these terrific books to your beginning-to-read collection."—*School Library Journal*

"A winner for the beginner."—*Booklist*

Five Tips to Help Your Child Become a Great Reader

1. Get involved. Reading aloud to and with your child is just as important as encouraging your child to read independently.

2. Be curious. Ask questions about what your child is reading.

3. Make reading fun. Allow your child to pick books on subjects that interest her or him.

4. Words are everywhere—not just in books. Practice reading signs, packages, and cereal boxes with your child.

5. Set a good example. Make sure your child sees YOU reading.

Why Green Light Readers Is the Best Series for Your New Reader

- Created exclusively for beginning readers by some of the biggest and brightest names in children's books

- Reinforces the reading skills your child is learning in school

- Encourages children to read—and finish—books by themselves

- Offers extra enrichment through fun, age-appropriate activities unique to each story

- Incorporates characteristics of the Reading Recovery program used by educators

- Developed with Harcourt School Publishers and credentialed educational consultants